The Cake that Mack Ate

To Darrell
He takes the cake

Kids Can Press Ltd. gratefully acknowledges the
assistance of the Canada Council and the Ontario
Arts Council in the production of this book.

Canadian Cataloguing in Publication Data
Robart, Rose.
The cake that Mack ate

ISBN 0-919964-96-6 (bound) ISBN 0-921103-29-8 (pbk.)

I. Kovalski, Maryann. II. Title.
PS8585.022C35 1986 jC811.54 C86-093467-5
PZ8.3.R63Ca 1986

Kids Can Press Ltd.,
585½ Bloor Street West,
Toronto, Ontario, Canada, M6G 1K5.

Book design by Michael Solomon
and Maryann Kovalski
Printed by Everbest Printing Co., Ltd., Hong Kong

PA 88 0 9 8 7 6 5 4 3 2 1

The Cake that Mack Ate

WRITTEN BY Rose Robart

ILLUSTRATED BY Maryann Kovalski

Kids Can Press Ltd.

Toronto

This is the cake
that Mack ate.

This is the egg
That went into the cake
that Mack ate.

This is the hen
That laid the egg,
That went into the cake
that Mack ate.

This is the corn
That fed the hen,
That laid the egg,
That went into the cake
that Mack ate.

This is the seed
That grew into corn,
That fed the hen,
That laid the egg,
That went into the cake
    that Mack ate.

This is the farmer
Who planted the seed,
That grew into corn,
That fed the hen,
That laid the egg,
That went into the cake
    that Mack ate.

This is the woman
Who married the farmer,
Who planted the seed,
That grew into corn,
That fed the hen,
That laid the egg,
That went into the cake
    that Mack ate.

These are the candles
That lit up the cake,
That was made by the woman,
Who married the farmer,
Who planted the seed,
That grew into corn,
That fed the hen,
That laid the egg,
That went into the cake
     that Mack ate.

This is Mack . . .

He ate the cake.